Patrick F. Kelly

Captain Kelly's Knapsack

well packed with a choice selection of his most popular songs and other

small pieces

Patrick F. Kelly

Captain Kelly's Knapsack
well packed with a choice selection of his most popular songs and other small pieces

ISBN/EAN: 9783337091743

Printed in Europe, USA, Canada, Australia, Japan

Cover: Foto ©Andreas Hilbeck / pixelio.de

More available books at **www.hansebooks.com**

Capt. Kelly's

N.Y.S VOL'S

Knapsack.

Respectfully Yours
Patrick F. Kelly

CONTENTS

OF

CAPTAIN KELLY'S KNAPSACK.

CONTENTS. —Concluded.

TO THE PUBLIC.

At the request of many friends, I have concluded to publish my war songs and other pieces, which I have written from time to time during my leisure moments. I gave some to the press and they were favorably received, which gives me confidence in my humble efforts to try again for public favor; and besides, my friends keep urging me on, as they claim I have some ability and ought to develop it. Some of them are so enthusiastic over my little pieces that they call me the "Bobby Burns" and "Tom Moore" of New York City, and my comrades of the late war call me the "Poet Laureate" of the G. A. R. If undeserved praise from my friends amounts to anything, I get plenty of it. I tell them they want to give me "taffy" and take it as a "fake." They cannot tickle my fancy with any such nonsense. Burns and Moore I honor and cherish their memory, and often talk with them through their works and take pleasure in doing so. We cannot all be great poets in this world and I don't propose to rub up against them; but I do think every man can do some good in this world, to show that he has lived for some purpose and try and leave something behind as a remembrance, and if my little pieces will be the means of instilling patriotism and love of country in our future rulers—the rising generation, I will be satisfied. We ought to leave a good record to them, to show them how much we loved our flag and country. Genius is like angel visits, few and far between. I confess that I have ambition to be remembered when I am gone to a brighter and better world, and if I have not the genius, I have the will to leave something worth preserving. I also trust whatever faults or errors the reader may find will be forgiven, and the will may be taken for the deed. In looking through my KNAPSACK you will find I give a little assortment, as variety is the spice of life, you can help yourself. Like all old vets, I have packed my Knapsack with odds and ends; my object is to please if possible, anyhow it is the best I can do, my motto is : " Do the best you can and help yourself," so I throw myself on the mercy of my old comrades, and the readers of my little book. I tried to bring some remembrance of the camp and field, when we were Uncle Sam's vets on eleven dollars per month, board and lodging, and living on the fat of the land, pork, junk and hard tack, and plenty of fresh air, with room enough to kick and grumble, when we felt like it, and if we did not like the bill of fare, we could do our own marketing, and go foraging, which we often did, the price of pigs and poultry made no difference to us when we went on a scout, we most always found something in the line of grub. The Lord helps those that help themselves; we understand enough of Scripture to help ourselves when hungry, and a change of diet was good for the system, so we had to keep our system right and be in fighting trim. Another good old maxim is : " As we journey through life, let us live by the way." Well, boys, we that are left ought to thank God we are living, after the many dangers and hardships we went through · I am speaking of the boys who enlisted in 1861 and 1862, who went at Lincoln's first call, for love of country and eleven dollars per month, before bounties were given. These men are the true heroes of the Union, and by all well thinking men are considered such. There are a few left who answered Lincoln's first call, and I am proud I am one of the few left, I served from May, 1861 until July, 1864, was promoted on the field and mustered out as Brevet Captain commanding company : twelve men left of 150 recruits, that's all, and I am willing to stay as long as the Lord will let me, and won't grumble neither if I am here when old Gabriel blows his horn and sounds the reveille. Well, my old comrades, we have done our duty, and it gives us pleasure to think we have lived for some good purpose in benefitting our fellow-men, and placing our country in its present proud position.

With these few remarks, I will say something of myself.

Shakespeare tells us some men are born great, and some are born with a silver spoon in their mouth. I was born young and handsome and never had a silver spoon, and don't want any. I am modest and can get along without them, corned beef and cabbage is good enough for me. I was always good natured, and willing to take a back seat and let others get in front, that is the reason I generally get left, but now too late, I am screwing my courage to the sticking point and may come to the front yet. My motto is : " Never despair," there is always room on top, and if a fellow keeps on climbing he will get above some of his neighbors. There is nothing like trying. I was a nice little cherub, into every mischief when growing up. I was sent to school when about seven years old, but the teachers and I could never agree. They said I was unruly and mischievous and would not learn, and I guess they were right. They used the rattan and ruler on me to bring me to terms, as they called it : but it did not have the desired effect on me, which I often since regretted. In those days the teachers used to lay it on pretty thick, and I do think if we had more of it now, it would improve the morals of the rising generation. Anyway, I did not take their advice, and they did not lick any learning into me, all I got is what I learned since I grew up, and that was very little. All I cared for was playing hookey, and going out to Sandy Gibson's and running to fires. Every boy in those days had their favorite machine to run with, and I had mine, in fact, I began to run to fires as soon as I wore pants. It was the joy of my life. When about ten years of age, I had the great misfortune to lose my parents ; then my troubles commenced. Left without a guide and protector so young, I grew up a little wild. I had to earn my living, and started in the newspaper business ; with a heavy heart and a few shillings in my pocket, I came in contact with some of the ablest and best men in the profession, and they all seemed to like me and take an interest in my welfare ; Horace Greeley, *Tribune*, James Gordon Bennett, *Herald*, and Moses Y. Beach, *Sun*. I recall with pleasure the good advice of the sage and philosopher, Horace Greeley, about leading a good temperate life, save my money and become a good and useful citizen. In fact, it was through Horace Greeley's teachings I became a teetotaler, I took the pledge of that great apostle of temperance Father Mathew, in 1849, which I still hold and will the remainder of my life. I served my country during the rebellion, from May 1861 until July 1864, continually in the field. I had all kinds of fevers ; took a hat full of quinine, in pills and powders, and never found an excuse for drinking. I was promoted from the ranks. I have two honorable discharges, and still hold the fort, and I must say, the young lads that were with me when I took the pledge, laughed and made fun of me, have all cashed in long ago; some of them before they were thirty years old, and all their prospects in life were brighter than mine. They had good fathers and mothers, and good homes and everything that love and money could give, while I had to battle through life and push ahead on my own hook and make friends as I went along, and I must say, that if a young man is sober and honest, he will make friends wherever he goes and will always find good men to assist him.

Well, comrades we have had our day, and are going fast, dropping like ripe fruit in bunches, and only a few are left to tell of the past We have done good in our day and feel proud of it. We have seen plenty of fun and glory, and that is worth thinking of and cheer us on the remainder of our days. I have tried to give a good moral in my songs and pieces, and if my readers find them interesting, and can spend a few pleasant moments in looking through my KNAPSACK, I hope they will think kindly of the author, who has tried to please them, and to spend a few pleasant moments in living our youth over again, and recalling recollections of the past, when we marched shoulder to shoulder and drank from the same canteen.

With these few remarks, and kind regards to all the Boys in Blue and all friends, I will say good-bye.

Your obedient servant,

PATRICK FRANCIS KELLY.

CAPTAIN KELLY'S KNAPSACK.

G. A. R. BADGE.

Respectfully dedicated to my Comrades in the G. A. R.

Capt. P. KELLY.

THE little Badge, I proudly bear,
    And have the right to wear it ;
Each comrade, now the glories share
    This token of great merit.

It tells of hardships in the Field,
    Where oft we fought together,
And in the shock of Battle reeled
    Each comrade was a brother.

It speaks of deeds and valor done
    On both the land and water,
Of Battles fought and victories won,
    Of deeds of fame and slaughter.

Boys, come and gather round our flag,
    And by the gods we swear it,
No foe shall live to boast or brag,
    To dim one star or tear it.

The Stars and Stripes, long may it wave,
    Naught can our Union sever ;
Over the land we fought to save,
    Oh, may it wave for ever.

OUR FLAG.

Respectfully dedicated to the G. A. R. and Veterans of the late War

By Capt. P. KELLY.

Our Starry Banner waves on high,
　A flag without a stain,
In freedom's cause will ever fly
　And peerless will remain ;
Its loving folds now all embrace,
　Like brothers we unite ;
No sections, hate no creed or race.
　No color, black or white.

Foul anarchy and Europe's dregs
　We will not tolerate,
No social forms in filth and rags,
　A burden on our State ;
With open heart and willing hand
　We welcome to our shore,
And greet them all to our fair land,
　The honest, brave and poor.

No dumping ground for serfs or slaves,
　Our flag is for the free,
Made sacred by the blood of braves,
　Who died for liberty ;

OUR FLAG.—Concluded.

And glorious sons of noble sires,
  Swear by the living God,
Our soil is free till time expires,
  No slave shall tread our sod.

Bold patriots, to win a name
  With the immortal band,
Will battle on with sword and flame
  For love of native land.
My country's flag, long may you wave,
  The emblem of the free,
I'd rush to glory or the grave,
  Old Flag for love of Thee.

MY OLD COMRADES.

Respectfully dedicated to the Veterans of the late War.

By Capt. P. KELLY.

BRAVE comrades all who wore the Blue,
Each gallant heart so firm and true,
Who nobly fought where many fell,
Amidst the strife of shot and shell,
With wild Hurrah 'gainst Rebel yell,
        My Old Comrades.

In bloom of youth and manhood pride,
When we were fighting side by side,
Hand to hand in many a fray
In rifle pits and trenches lay,
And stopping balls that came our way,
        My Old Comrades.

MY OLD COMRADES.—Concluded.

We're growing old, our days gone by,
No place for us, no use to try ;
A poor old Vet has got no show,
Bum Politicians, all the go,
And fellows never struck a blow,
                    My Old Comrades.

There is no place for you or me,
In our fair land we helped to free ;
For Politicians got the rake
And give old Vets a dirty shake,
They grab up all, and take the cake,
                    My Old Comrades.

But when our country needed men,
Loyal and true with sword and pen ;
When treason with its guilty hand
Spread desolation through our land,
The boys in Blue, were in demand,
                    My Old Comrades.

No bugle blast now strikes the ear,
And clash of arms, no more we hear ;
From North to South, our land is free,
Rid of the curse of slavery,
The color line no more we see,
                    My Old Comrades.

The Union saved, our work is done,
Rest on the laurels nobly won ;
Sing anthems for our gallant dead,
Who in the cause of freedom bled,
With garlands deck each heroes bed,
                    My Old Comrades.

THE GRAND POTOMAC ARMY.

Respectfully dedicated to the G. A. R. and Comrades of the late War

By Capt. P. Kelly.

BRAVE Comrades, join me in three cheers,
And wipe away all bitter tears,
That wet our cheeks for many years
    In the Grand Potomac Army.
We give our heart and hand to those
Who met us in the field as foes,
Our malice ended with our blows,
    In the Grand Potomac Army.
Peace and good-will we cherish still,
    In the Grand Potomac Army.

To all who nobly led the van,
Our glorious GRANT and SHERIDAN,
In freedom's cause to every man,
    Of the Grand Potomac Army.
To little Mac, the soldier's pride,
And gallant Meade, the true and tried,
To fighting Joe, and brave Burnside,
    Of the Grand Po omac Army.
Each honored name will live in fame,
    Of the Grand Potomac Army.

Now smiling peace has come again,
No warrior's blood was shed in vain,
And glory crowns the fallen slain,
    Of the Grand Potomac Army.
Departed braves, the good and true,
Each gallant heart who wore the blue,
A laurel wreath we wave for you,
    Of the Grand Potomac Army.
Each passing year we prize more dear
    The Old Potomac Army.

LINCOLN'S ADDRESS.

TUNE—" Scots wha hae wi Wallace Bled."

By Capt. P. KELLY.

WHEN traitors fired on our flag,
Then did make their boast and brag,
Stars and Bars would be the rag
        Of Southern chivalry.

Their cursed work, they first begun,
On Sumter's walls, near Charleston,
Defended by Brave Anderson,
        With Spartan bravery.

Every means they sought and tried
Our glorious Union to divide,
Seized our ships and laws defied
        To rend our unity.

They trampled all was good and just,
Our Starry Flag trailed in the dust,
And Soldiers into prison thrust,
        And Union men to flee.

Freemen, aroused, armed for the fray,
To wipe foul treason stains away,
Thank God we live to see the day
        Bring peace and victory.

A Nation mourns her fallen slain,
Who died for freedom, not in vain,
They broke the captives galling chain,
        And set the bondman free.

OLD LANG SYNE.

To be sung at Camp Fires and Meetings of Old Veterans.

Respectfully dedicated to the G. A. R.

By Capt. P. KELLY.

BRAVE comrades now we meet again—
The Field, Staff, and the Line ;
Your glasses, boys, come fill and drain,
We drink to Old Lang Syne.

CHORUS.

Come, put it here—a good old shake—
Your honest hand in mine :
Now, fill your glasses, touch and take ;
We drink to Old Lang Syne.

Drink to our gallant rank and file ;
They came from every clime,
And met grim death, boys, with a smile,
In days of Old Lang Syne.

Chorus—Come, put it here.

We drink now to departed braves—
God's memory on them shine—
The Nation's wards in honored graves,
For days of Old Lang Syne.

Chorus—Come, put it here.

OLD LANG SYNE.—Concluded.

The Stars and Stripes will ever be
    Our old flag—yours and mine ;
We hail it, boys, with three times three,
    For days of Old Lang Syne.
            Chorus—Come, put it here

Hardtack and Pork we had enough—
    On woodcock now we dine ;
Brave Boys, you know we had it rough
    In days of Old Lang Syne.
            Chorus—Come, put it here.

Before we part, our pledge renew,
    To meet another time,
The friends we love so warm and true ;
    We meet for Old Lang Syne.
            Chorus—Come, put it here.

Boys, marching orders soon will come :
    We all must fall in line,
With arms reversed, and muffled drum,
    Farewell to Old Lang Syne.
            Chorus—All hands round.

Come, put it here—a good old shake—
    Your honest hand in mine ;
All fill your glasses, touch and take ;
    We drink to Old Lang Syne.

RED, WHITE AND BLUE.

Respectfully dedicated to my old Comrades and Veterans
of the late War.

By Capt. P. KELLY.

At Lincoln's loud call in the year sixty-one,
W.aen every brave freeman and true-hearted son
Then shouldered his rifle, to home bade adieu,
To fight for the Union, the Red, White and Blue.

CHORUS.

We marched away, marched like heroes so true—
To all fight and die for the Red, White and Blue.

In camp or on marches, by day or by night,
Our brave boys were ready to battle for right ;
The bondsman, a chattel, for freedom did sue,
We fought for his ransom, the Red, White and Blue.

CHORUS.

All day we go scouting o'er fields and through wood,
And sometimes are up to our knees in the mud,
Without any rations, and barefooted to—
We'll all die defending the Red, White and Blue.

CHORUS.

When night comes we station our pickets around,
Then roll in our blankets and sleep on the ground ;
The loved ones at home in visions we view,
While guarding the Union, the Red, White and Blue

CHORUS.

We rise in the morning before break of day,
Eat hardtack and coffee, and then march away,

RED, WHITE AND BLUE.—Concluded.

After the "Johnnies" we're bound to subdue,
And make them submit to the Red, White and Blue.

CHORUS.

I've been in the army for over three years,
And fought for the Union with brave volunteers ;
I've seen some hard fighting, and dangers went through,
Three cheers for the Union, the Red, White and Blue.

CHORUS.

We marched away, marched, like heroes so true—
Three cheers for the Union, the Red, White and Blue.

ACROSTIC.

To my Katie.

By Capt. P. Kelly

K indness, true friend-hip will impart,
A nd carries the joy to every heart
T o all alike brings sweet repose ;
I n sorrow, too, its fragrance shows
E 'en sweeter than the scented rose.

K eep truth and justice on your side,
E ver through life your safest guide ;
L et others sigh for wealth and fame.
L eave it to them ; "What's in a name ?"
Y our heart keeps pure—your soul the same.

ON THE DEATH OF ABRAHAM LINCOLN, OUR MARTYRED PRESIDENT.

By Capt. P. KELLY

GREAT Lincoln, Martyred President,
 In war-like strife and deadly hate,
A heavenly messenger was sent
 To guide our noble Ship of State ;
Thy glorious deeds are like a chart,
Engraven on each patriot's heart.

Our Lord had chosen him to guide,
 And all revere his honored name ;
The Nation's bulwark, hope and pride,
 Time brightens his undying fame ;
Like Moses through the dark Red Sea
Led captives from captivity.

From rugged toil and lowly birth,
 With genius rare, and wit combined,
All Nation's now proclaim his worth
 A benefactor to mankind ;
He spent his stormy life's short span
To elevate his fellow man.

With tender heart and genial smile,
 Was ever prompt at duty's call,
With pleasant tales the hours beguile,
 And charity and love for all ;
One of the kindest, best of men,
 We ne'er shall see his like again.

Cursed be the hand that laid thee low,
 The greatest, noblest of mankind ;
May curses deep as torrents flow

ON THE DEATH OF ABRAHAM LINCOLN, OUR MARTYRED PRESIDENT.—Concluded.

On the base wretches who combined,
   With murder, foul, and treason's sway
   The right of freedom to betray.

Base rebels, struggled to divide
   The finest structure man e'er built—
Spread desolation far and wide
   In blackest crimes of blood and guilt ;
And our fair land for four long years,
   Was drenched in sorrow, blood and tears.

At Appomatox where the sun
   Of reason set to rise no more ;
Now lights up freedom's horizon,
   On fields and meadows soaked in gore ;
Where brothers met in deadly fray,
   Misguided men who wore the gray.

Lincoln and Grant will ever be
   Immortal names not born to die,
The watchword of the brave and free,
   In loud Hosannas to the sky ;
Lincoln the ruler, wise and great,
   And Grant the Saviour of the State.

May cruel war and hatred cease,
   And brotherhood of man combine,
Extend the olive branch of peace
   With love and charity entwine ;
Around the hearts and soul of men,
   And fight all battles with the pen.

SHENANDOAH.

General P. H. Sheridan, the bravest of the brave. He plucked victory
from defeat. Never lost a battle

By Capt. P. KELLY.

BRAVE SHERIDAN, first in the van,
    To lead his men to victory ;
So bold and grand, born to command,
    The pride and flower of chivalry.

Brave son of Mars won his gold stars
    On fields of blood and glory—
His honored name shines bright in fame,
    Will live in song and story.

At Shenandoah, he met the foe,
    Gave them no time to rally ;
With sabre stroke, through flame and smoke,
    He drove them from the valley.

With sudden dash, quick as a flash,
    Came down on them like thunder—
The charge he made o'er hill and glade,
    Caused all the world to wonder.

Oh ! mighty chief, thy years were brief,
    No time or space can sever ;
Fame's gallant son, your race is run,
    Your deeds will live for ever.

Comrades, we will all drink to Phil,
    Our darling little fighter ;
God rest his soul, may he enroll
    In fields more fair and brighter.

THE GALLANT NINETY-NINE.

Most respectfully dedicated to my old Comrades of the Ninety-Ninth
Regiment, New York Volunteers.

By Capt. P. KELLY.

BRAVE comrades, all, come list to me, your spirits I will cheer,
And try and sing the praise of the gallant volunteer ;
On picket guard or fighting, boys, with spirits gay and fine;
I do declare, few can compare with gallant Ninety-Nine.

At Big Bethel and Newmarket Bridge, we tried the rebel
    pluck,
At Hampton Roads, our boys were there and to their colors
    stuck :
Our lads on board the " Congress," with valor there did shine,
And work'd their guns like noble sons of gallant Ninety-Nine.

Our brave boys were at Hatteras, Roanoke and Newbern,
To Norfolk next, we then did go, to give them another turn;
We landed at Cape Henry, on the beach we formed in line,
Hurrah ! they come with fife and drum, the gallant Ninety-
    Nine.

At Norfolk then we did encamp, for near six months we lay,
Then to Deep Creek we started off to drive the rebels away;
Through rain and mud we march'd along o'er trees of fallen
    pine ;
The rebs retire from the fire of gallant Ninety-Nine.

To Suffolk next we then did go, and left our camping ground,
Now ordered to the front brave boys, the rebs did us
    surround ;
For three weeks in the trenches lay, in weather, rain or shine;
In the rifle pits we gave them fits ; Hurrah for Ninety Nine

THE GALLANT NINETY-NINE.—Concluded.

We lost many gallant comrades, boys, on the first of May,
Sad to relate, our loss was great in that bloody fray ;
Full sixty killed and wounded, fell out of the line ;
We drop a tear to memory dear, the killed of Ninety-Nine.

The flowers bloom now o'er the tomb of our departed brave,
And sad to tell, brave Hart* he fell, and fills a soldier's grave ;
On the Blackwater ford his men deployed, as skirmishers in
 line,
A rebel sent a ball that went through brave Hart of Ninety-
 Nine.

* The writer's old captain, J. H. Hart, of Co. E. 99th N. Y. S. Vols.,
killed June 16th, 1863.

ON THE LATE SENATOR JOHN MORRISSEY

A small tribute of respect to his memory, by one who admired his
many noble qualities while living, and now mourns his early death.
Capt. P. KELLY.

J ust, generous, so brave and true,
O h, worthy chief, with pride we scan ;
H ow short thy years—alas, too few,
N oble and great, an honest man.

M ay perpetual light, forever shine
O n thy poor servant passed away—
R aise him, oh Lord, to joys divine,
R obed in the light of Heavenly day ;
I n Thee he placed his hope and trust,
S weet Jesus, let thy mercy flow,
S aved by thy grace, thy ways are just,
E ternal bliss on him bestow;
Y our boundless love unto him show.

LINES ON THE LATE GENERAL JAMES McQUADE.

A gallant soldier and Past State Commander of the G. A. R.

By Capt. P. KELLY.

A SOLDIER, comrade and a friend,
A man of fame and sterling worth ;
One of the few that Heaven sent
To make it brighter here on earth ;
And nature's masterpiece was made
When you were finished, James McQuade.

When battle raged most fierce and wild,
And treason foul our land o'erspread ;
When on each gory field lay piled
In heaps, the dying and the dead ;
Then leading on your old Brigade
You gain'd new laurels, James McQuade.

With noble heart, and gifted mind,
His hand was free to aid distress—
A brother was to all mankind,
To give relief, to cheer and bless ;
And to assist a poor comrade,
Was always ready, James McQuade.

Our heroes die, the best are gone,
The brightest flowers soon will fade ;
Their deeds will live, without a stone
To mark the spot where they are laid ;
Logan, our pride and true comrade
Is mustered out with James McQuade.

LINES ON THE LATE GENERAL JAMES McQUADE.—Concluded.

We're going fast as time rolls by,
Our comrades, dropping day by day,
Death severs every kindred tie,
Our ranks grow thin and waste away ;
Brave Grant and Sheridan are laid
To rest with Hancock and McQuade.

When we assemble up on high,
And in bright robes will be arrayed,
In glory's ranks beyond the sky,
And all fall in for dress parade,
To mingle in one social grade
In Heaven, above, with James McQuade.

ODE TO BUNKER HILL.

The author while on to Boston to the National Encampment of the
G. A. R., visited some of the Historical places in and around Boston,
and composed the following lines.

Capt. P. KELLY.

AMID the glories of the past,
    I fondly love to dwell,
Where freedom's sky was overcast,
    And patriots fought so well ;
In reverence and awe did stand
    Beneath the old Elm tree,
Where Washington first took command
    To fight for liberty

ODE TO BUNKER HILL.—Concluded.

I stood upon famed Bunker Hill,
  Where gallant Warren fell,
And mused upon the ground until
  My heart with rapture's swell ;
The holy pride that freedom gives,
  Inspires the mind and will,
And proves the same old spirit lives
  That fought at Bunker Hill.

With thoughts that burn and words of fire
  In grand old Faneuil Hall,
Bold patriots with vengeance dire,
  Rallied at freedom's call ;
They lit a torch throughout the world,
  The fires are blazing still,
And tyrants in the dust were hurled
  On famous Bunker hill.

At Concord and at Lexington,
  The glorious strife began,
And there bequeathed from sire to son,
  Freedom, the rights of man ;
To old King George, they owed a debt,
  And well they paid the bill,
For all mankind are praising yet
  That day on Bunker Hill.

Long live the memory of the dead
  Who died for liberty ;
May freedom's cause forever spread
  Till all enslaved are free ;
May serfs and slaves take up the cry.
  The God of battles will,
And angels will rejoice on high
  For deeds like Bunker Hill.

CAMP AND FIELD.

Written for the 25th Anniversary of Phil. Kearney Post
N. Y., G. A. R.

By Capt. P. KELLY.

PHIL. KEARNEY boys, welcome to-night,
With hearts so loyal, true and light ;
    Comrades who wore the Blue.
And shared the dangers of the past,
Answered the call of bugle blast,
    The long roll and tat-too.

Touched elbows in the march and strife
When we were battling for dear life,
    O'er fields and meadows green.
Our Nation's bulwarks and her pride,
When we were fighting side by side,
    Drank from the same canteen.

Bold Kearney, of chivalric race,
The saddle was the hero's place ;
    His honored name we bear.
Amid the cannon deadly peal,
Through shot, and shell, and gleaming steel,
    On dashed our cavalier.

That fated night of Chantilly,
We lost the flower of chivalry.
    The night was drear and dark.
With reins grasp'd tight between his teeth,
He rode right in the jaws of death;
    Death loves a shining mark.

CAMP AND FIELD.—Continued.

We had as guest our comrade Dan,
At Gettysburg was in the van;
      Our Sickles led the way.
With his heroic blood he sealed
Upon that famous and gory field,
      His valor saved the day.

With honor crown'd and weight of years,
Our brave old comrade still appears
      A soldier, true and brave.
With martial bearing, purpose grand,
A famous hero now does stand
      With one foot in the grave.

Give all the boys their mete of praise,
They fought like h'll in those dark days,
      And every time to win.
Oh ! what a grand and solemn sight
For God, our country, and for right,
      To see the boys go in.

With head erect, and cheery song,
How oft we passed the days along,
      No dangers could appall.
As forward in the fight we press,
No one could tell or give a guess
      The next comrade to fall.

Old shipmates, now, can have their say,
Of battles won, and well they may;
      They fought and died like braves.
Their guns pealed forth like thunder clouds,
Brave Farragut lashed to the shrouds ;
      The ruler of the waves.

CAMP AND FIELD.—Concluded.

The tough old vets who still remain,
Oft fight their battles o'er again,
   How comrades fought and fell.
And talk of days of Old Lang Syne,
Hard fighting on the picket line,
   The zip of shot and shell.

Our boys did forage, now and then,
Chickens are good for hungry men ;
   I think them bully fare.
We all found them a great relief
From rotten pork and stinking beef ;
   I know it ; I've been there.

We had some sneaks and copperheads,
Lived on good feed and feather beds,
   When we lay in the mud.
And our poor teeth and jaws did crack
On old salt horse and mouldy tack—
   D—m them, they are no good.

Now as our years and cares increase,
We smoke the pipe of love and peace,
   And think of days gone by.
When we dodged balls upon the wing,
Just as the bees do buzz and sing,
   When they are on the fly.

We tramp no more on march or scout,
Soon taps will sound and lights go out,
   Our days are short and few.
The Lord is good and will provide
A nice place on the other side—
   For all the boys in blue.

MEMORIAL DAY IN CALVARY.

In memory of our dead who rest there for service on Memorial Day.

By Capt. P. KELLY.

WE'RE treading now on Hallowed ground,
'Midst joys and hopes lie buried here;
Each little plot and grassy mound
Is sanctified to memory dear.
Fond hearts I loved, and true to me,
Are resting here in Calvary.

The soldier who for country fell,
And heroes who came home to die
From wounds received by shot and shell,
Within this sacred spot they lie.
No more will answer reveille,
Their arms are stacked in Calvary.

Old comrades, they assemble here,
With friendship's offering to the brave,
The same sad rite each passing year,
To strew fresh flowers on each grave.
Those loving scenes I long to see
On Memorial day in Calvary.

The widow bowed in humble prayer,
And kneeling on the cold, damp sod,
Mourns for her husband resting here,
And praying to Almighty God.
For his poor soul! oh, may it be
With our dear Lord on Calvary.

Fond mothers, they come here to pray
And weep for loved ones dead and gone
In silent tears they pass the day,

MEMORIAL DAY IN CALVARY.—Concluded.

In grief and anguish sigh and moan.
Great God of love, they call on thee,
  And Christ, who died on Calvary.

The hardy sons of honest toil,
  Their deeds and virtues all unknown,
Lie buried in this sacred soil,
  Their praise unsung, without a stone.
Life's struggles bore with poverty,
  Like Christ, who died on Calvary.

We see the graves of pampered pride,
  With monuments rising to the skies ;
Their names and deeds are glorified
  To make them all that's good and wise.
Famed men of high and low degree,
  All are the same in Calvary.

Man lingers here a few short years,
  A pilgrim on life's busy stage,
With hopes and joys and many tears,
  Then drops into the silent grave.
Christ bore the cross for you and me,
  And conquered death on Calvary.

Oh God of mercy, love, and grace,
  Our only hope in life and death,
Protect and guide us all our days ;
  Be near us at our parting breath.
Thy mercy great, to all is free—
  Man's glory dates from Calvary.

DIRGE.

On the late General PHILIP H. SHERIDAN, one of the best generals
and greatest fighters the world ever saw.

TUNE—"The Harp That Once."

By Capt. P. KELLY.

Oh, sing a Requiem for the brave,
  We must bow to Heaven's will—
For glory's path leads to the grave,
  Fare thee well, our Gallant Phil.

Death has draped his sable plume
  'Round the dying soldier's bed,
And valor weeps now at the tomb
  Over the immortal dead.

The oak and laurel now entwine
  For the bravest and the best ;
And place a garland on the shrine
  Where our hero lies at rest.

Columbia mourns her gallant son
  While the stars shine in the sky ;
And while grass grows and waters run,
  Sheridan will never die.

Bright angels, in a golden car,
  Soaring to the starry skies,
Will open wide the gates ajar,
  And welcome him to paradise.

HYMN.

The Blue and Gray—a song of love and peace for Memorial Day.

By Capt. P. KELLY.

ALL quiet now along the line,
We fire no more to kill ;
And need no pass or countersign,
Are free to roam at will.
One flag and country now so grand,
And union rules the day,
Peace and content—a happy land
Reigns over Blue and Gray.

As years roll on, the deadly strife
Is buried in the past ;
When brother sought a brother's life,
And blood ran thick and fast ;
Oh ! may the peace that cost so dear,
Last on till endless day,
With charity and love sincere
Between the Blue and Gray.

We pray for friends, we pray for foes,
Thy mercy, Lord, we crave—
To heal our sorrows cares and woes,
Each precious soul to save ;
We sing to Thee, our anthems rise
To God, who rules above,
From earth, thy foot-stool to the skies.
A song of praise and love.

IN MEMORY OF MY BELOVED MOTHER.

By her affectionate son, Capt. P. KELLY.

In sweet remembrance still I trace
My mother's smile and gentle face,
Long numbered with the silent dead—
May holy angels guard her bed ;
Too good for earth to longer stay,
Bright seraphs l ore her soul away,
In life's great book, there to enroll
My mother dear, God rest her soul.

Her angel smile has gone from me,
My mother's face, no more will see ;
No more will hear her joyous song
To warm my heart and cheer me on.
Cast young adrift on life's dark sea,
No one to guide or care for me,
Without a chart for rock or shoal—
My mother dear, God rest her soul.

How oft you took me on your knee,
To teach me all I ought to be,
Mark out the road I should pursue,
Be kind to all, give each their due ;
Trust in the Lord, his word obey,
His blessing seek, and ask each day
On his great mercy to rely,
And look for wisdom from on high.

Reflect at night, think and survey
The actions, done throughout the day,
Then treasure up and nurse with care
The joys I would receive and share ;

IN MEMORY OF MY BELOVED MOTHER.
Concluded.

And thus the cheerful hours prolong
With counsel wise and loving song.
Life's busy cares and labors done,
You doted on your only son.

With holy faith and trust in God,
And hope in the Redeemer's blood,
You welcomed death to win the prize,
A glorious crown in Paradise.
How sweet your memory still appears,
Through the long flight of waning years.
God rest your soul, my mother dear,
Eternal Father hear my prayer.

EPITAPH.

May Heaven's portion be your bed,
    And all its joys to share it ;
A crown, dear mother, deck your head,
    In glory bright to wear it.

IN MEMORY OF MY GRANDSON, JAMES K. CONNELL.

AGED TWO YEARS AND FIVE MONTHS.

By Capt. P. KELLY.

Now, I linger hear and mourn
My poor heart does overflow,
And my breast does rack and burn
With a load of grief and woe ;

IN MEMORY OF MY GRANDSON, JAMES K. CONNELL.—Concluded.

Death has robbed us of our joy—
For his loss, I moan and sigh,
Our bright hope and lovely boy,
Farewell, darling Jim, good-bye.

Papa now in silence weeps
For the idol of his heart,
In the grave his baby sleeps,
Cruel death, tore them apart—
His fine boy was fair of face,
And the apple of his eye,
Grand and noble, full of grace,
Farewell, darling Jim, good-bye.

Mama bowed with grief and care,
As she ponders day by day
On her Jimmy's vacant chair,
Nature then asserts her sway.
Jesus called him for his own
To his mansions in the sky,
Plead for us, before his throne,
Farewell, darling Jim, good-bye.

Death will sorrow surely bring,
And the brightest mark will strike ;
Sure to leave a wound and sting
To the rich and poor alike.
God has willed it, so 't must be,
All mankind is born to die ;
We must bow to His decree,
Farewell, darling Jim, good-bye.

TO MY GRAND DAUGHTERS.

MARY, FRANCES AND ELEANOR LORETTA CONNELL.

(MY BLUE-EYED NELL AND BONNY MAY.)

By Capt. P. KELLY.

TUNE.—" My Nannie, Oh."

SWEET buds of promise, fair to view,
    Two cherubs of celestial ray ;
Christ taught and welcomed such as you,
    My Blue-eyed Nell and Bonny May.

No fairer rosebuds ever grew,
    Or poet sang to minstrel lay,
Or sunshine kiss'd with pearly dew,
    Than Blue-eyed Nell and Bonny May.

Lord fill your hearts with holy grace,
    And keep you safe each coming day ;
Shed blessings on your name and race,
    My Blue-eyed Nell and Bonny May.

My humble prayer to God ascend
    To be your guide and heavenly stay
On earth, your hope, through life, your friend
    My Blue-eyed Nell and Bonny May.

Sweet, lovely girls, my heart endears,
    And your best smiles now light the way ;
Brings joy to my declining years,
    My darling pets, sweet Nell and May.

IN MEMORY OF MY LOVING SISTER,

Winifred Henry.

By her loving brother, Capt. P. KELLY.

You sleep the sleep that knows no waking,
  Now life's fitful dream is o'er :
D ar children weep, your hearts are breaking,
  Mother's face will see no more.
A loving wife, kind friend and neighbor,
  In each sphere you bore your part—
Would for the sick and needy labor,
  With a kind and Christian heart.

Death has ended all your sorrow,
  To your faith and Saviour true,
For you there is no coming morrow,
  God be merciful to you.
The golden links that bound together
  Our fond hearts and made them one—
A loving sister and a brother—
  Broken now, God's will be done.

Your holy faith did cheer our sadness,
  Makes our sorrows light to bear ;
You welcomed death with joy and gladness,
  For the crown you hoped to wear.
Robed in white, your sins forgiven,
  Your poor soul, I trust is free,
With bright angels now in Heaven,
  Sister dear, we pray for thee.

TO MY ESTEEMED FRIEND, COLONEL

GEORGE BLISS.

By Capt. P. KELLY.

FRIEND BLISS, thy name will shine with grace,
Be honored by your clime and race
    As patriot and sage.
One of the great and noble men,
To draw the sword and yield the pen,
    When treason was the rage.

In peace and war, your country's stay,
A beacon light to guide the way,
    When clouds darkened our land.
And others faltered in the fight
For human justice and for right—
    You boldly took your stand.

A nestor of fair freedom's bar
And liberty's bright guiding star;
    An eagle on the wing.
In wisdom great and virtue strong
To shield the weak and right the wrong;
    Thy deeds I love to sing.

TO MY ESTEEMED FRIEND, COLONEL
GEORGE BLISS.—Concluded.

Thy generous heart to me was kind
Deep gratitude will ever bind
        The debt I owe to thee.
Thou art a friend, in word and deed,
I found thee a true friend in need,
        In love and charity.

I shared the sorrows and the strife,
The joys too, of this stormy life ;
        Its ups and downs I know.
But now, I trust, the clouds are past
And bright sunshine has come at last,
        To cheer me as I go.

'Till the cold icy hand of death
Shall stop my pulse and chill my breath,
        My thoughts will run to Thee.
My fervent prayer, for you George Bliss,
Long life, health, wealth and happiness,
        Where ever you may be.

God bless your kind and noble heart,
And may the Lord his grace impart
        Each boon to virtue given.
So when this busy life is done,
Your work is o'er and race is run,
        To your reward in Heaven

GOD HELP THE NEEDY POOR.

Respectfully dedicated to the Knights of Labor.

TUNE—"The Wearing of the Green."

By Capt P. KELLY.

THE times are hard, and all complain,
 What can a poor man do ?
Business dull, shops closed again,
 Work only for a few.
Our wives and children cry for bread—
 Grim want is at our door ;
We struggle on till hope has fled—
 God help the needy poor.

How hard the miseries of life
 The poor man has to share ;
The trials, sufferings and the strife,
 The burdens other than we bear ;
Misfortune follows woe and want,
 We suffer and endure,
And labor hard, our pay is scant—
 God help the needy poor.

Now, poverty is not a crime,
 And should be no disgrace,
The men of wealth in every clime
 Should share it with their race,
And freely give, with heart and hand,

GOD HELP THE NEEDY POOR.—Concluded.

From out their worldly store ;
All should obey divine command :
Go feed and clothe the poor.

Proud capital, it will combine
To raise both food and rent,
And everything man needs in fine,
Each gift that God has sent—
Men hoard up wealth, with millions play,
Will feast and squander more,
While poor are starving day by day,
God help the starving poor.

Brave noblemen, our country's pride
And hope in time of need,
The bone and sinew, true and tried,
In freedom's cause you lead ;
Defender's of our flag and soil,
The flag we all adore,
Hard-fisted sons of honest toil,
The fearless, brave and poor.

We look to Him who rules on high,
Great God above us all ;
He hears the widow's mournful cry,
And sees the sparrow's fall,
Shelters the orphan in distress,
The lowly and obscure ;
The saints all praise and angels bless,
God will reward the poor.

TO MY FRIEND CHARLES SHAY,

The Popular Foreman of 14 Engine.

By Capt. P. KELLY.

My sunny days are rolling by,
But still my heart is light and gay ;
I'll catch some pleasure on the fly,
Before I go, dear Charley Shay.

We're pilgrims on life's dreary road—
And only here a while to stay ;
Care and old age, a heavy load,
Will knock us out, dear Charley Shay.

Then come, enjoy each passing hour,
This life is frail and made of clay ;
Our time is short and like a flower,
We droop and fade, dear Charley Shay.

Then, thank the Lord for favors past,
And all he sends each coming day ;
And may his mercies ever last
To us, poor sinners, Charley Shay.

God bless you boy, where e'er you be,
May fortune follow where you stray—
In foreign lands or stormy sea,
My blessing with you, Charley Shay.

THE GALLANT FIREMEN.

Respectfully dedicated to the members of the New York Fire
Department, preservers of our lives and property.

By Capt. P. KELLY.

THE gallant firemen, bold and true,
  Are ever prompt on duty's call ;
Our lives and hopes depend on you,
  No fear of death your minds appall.
When flames roll out and flames arise
To fight a pathway to the skies,
Then summoned by the bell or wire,
Where duty calls to save from fire.

CHORUS.

The bells .ing out, and call for aid,
  And steady runs the clinking wire :
Bold heroes of the fire brigade,
  Turn out ! turn out, boys ! Fire ! fire !

Midst flames and smoke we see you stand,
  And while the sparks around you fly,
Battling for life with pipe in hand,
  The terrors of grim death defy ;
Your life's great hope and only aim
  To rescue from the burning flame ;
Your deeds of valor all admire
  When duty calls to save from fire.
      Chorus—The bells ring out and call.

May God protect and spare your lives,
  Bold heroes of the fire brigade,
To kindred, home, and loving wives,
  And may your laurels never fade,
May friendship smile, and gentle love
  Warm each stout heart, till call'd above.
In doing good you never tire
  When duty calls to save from fire.
      Chorus—The bells ring out and call.

OUR BRAVE POLICEMEN.

A small tribute of respect to our guardians of the peace, who risk
their lives in preserving law and order.

By Capt. P. KELLY.

In shades of night, when all is still,
And drowsy sleep the eyelids fill ;
When crime and guilt, which fear the light,
Steals on its victims in the night,
The worthy chief, in order brief,
Sends forth his men to find the thief.

All rogues and thieves, like beasts of prey,
Will rob and steal, then sneak away,
And if pursued, will take a life
With pistol, club, or deadly knife.
The heart will bleed at some foul deed
By frenzied man for gain or greed.

Men branded with the mark of Cain,
With blood their guilty souls will stain ;
Will spend their lives to plot or plan
'Gainst all the laws of God and man.
The police trace each hardened case—
Those vampires of the human race.

Swift justice; like an eagle's flight,
The blackest crimes will bring to light—
Track felons to the gates of hell,
And lodge them in a prison cell.
They find a clue and will pursue
The rascals till they get their due.

On brave policemen all depend
To guard our homes and lives defend ;
Fearless and brave, and ever true,
The public welfare keep in view.
Through rain and snow on watch they go,
A mark for the assassin's blow.

OLD FIRE LADDIE.

Respectfully dedicated to the members of the Old Volunteer Fire
Department, of New York City, as a testimony of their worth
and zeal in devoting their lives and services in rescuing the lives
and property of their fellow citizens, without pay or reward.
The author passed many pleasant days in their company.

By Capt. P. KELLY.

TUNE.—"The Wearing of the Green."

My thoughts oft wander to the time when it was joy to me
To hear the old firebell ring out ; what pleasure then to see
Our laddies rushing at the sound, and running to a fire ;
Before the days of steam I sing, or telegraphic wire.

Our noble lads, when duty called, no dangers did they fear;
They went to rescue and to save, a gallant volunteer.
Red shirt, dark pants, a belt and cap, their rig a gay attire ·
You bet they made things lively, boys, when running to a fire.

The bell had music in its tone, it charmed the hearts of all ;
Our boys dropp'd work and business too in answer to the
    call,
Their services to the public free, they asked no pay or hire ;
Without reward they risked their lives to rescue from the fire.

OLD FIRE LADDIE.—Continued.

Their brawny arms did man the brakes, and make the
water fly ;
'Twas fun to wash some boss machine, and suck another dry;
And if the boys fooled with the butt, or gave us any chin,
Our lads were pretty handy, on their muscle did sail in.

I like to sit around and hear the old boys laugh and tell
The time they passed some fast machine, and went by with
a yell,
And how they spun along the track, through rain, hail, snow
and mire,
What time they made a getting in, put first stream on the
fire.   •

Sometimes I meet, and glad to see some of the old stock
left,
How many more we miss, brave boys, are sleeping cold in
death.
The fleeting years go rolling by, we're getting bald and
• gray ;
Most of the lads have all cash'd in, and we are on the way.

We gather round, recall the past, and list to some dear
name,
Who gave his life, at duty's call, to save from smoke and
flame ;
Who onward to the rescue went, a helpless life to save,
Through blinding smoke and falling walls, and filled a
martyr's grave.

OLD FIRE LADDIE.—Concluded.

How times have changed, and now we have another race
    of men ;
The boys now gone, we never more will see their like again.
Brave, noble lads, so firm and true, your records plainly
    tell ;
Your gallant deeds will ever live. Brave boys, a long
    farewell.

TO MY LOVING DAUGHTER C. B. CONNELL.

By Capt. P. KELLY.

My bonny Kate is like a fairy,
    Dear to me, so blithe and gay ;
With form so fair, step light and airy ;
    Sweeter than the rose in May.

Nut brown is her waving tresses,
    Bright as sunlight is her eye ;
And loving heart to cheer and bless us,
    Beaming like a summer sky.

Her gentle heart is warm and tender,
    Pure in thought and free from guile,
And mine a thrill of joy doth render,
    As I greet her winning smile.

In Katie lies my hope and treasure,
    For great bliss her smiles impart ;
My Katie is my pride and pleasure,
    As I fold her to my heart.

FORTY YEARS AGO.

By Capt. P. KELLY.

How times have changed since we were boys,
    Some forty years ago ;
The youngsters now are very fast,
    And say our pace is slow ;
Old Time does rock the boys to sleep,
    To pay the debt we owe ;
The good old stock is dying out
    Since forty years ago.

What bully times at Sandy's, boys !
    Those days are past and gone ;
And when our rations did run short,
    Strike in for Copey John.
No sorrow then or care we knew,
    No trouble, grief or woe,
For everything was lovely, boys,
    Some forty years ago.

How many ups and downs in life,
    What sport too we have seen,
And when the old firebell rung out,
    To run with the machine ;
And if we had a little muss,
    It ended with a blow—
Our bully boys would use no knives
    Some forty years ago.

My poor old pate is getting bald,
    The few hairs left are gray,
And, like the good old times we had,
    The rest will pass away.
The boys are scattered far and wide—
    Tom, Billy, Mike and Joe—
And for their country many died
    Since forty years ago.

VETERAN'S DREAM.

Respectfully dedicated to the Veterans of the late War.

By Capt. P. Kelly.

By George, I had a pleasant dream
  The other night in bed ;
In blissful fancy, I did seem,
  Methought that I was dead ,
And left all cares of worldly state
  To meet Saint Peter at the gate.

When I got there Saint Peter cried :
  Now, where from down below ?
Come, show your passport, stand aside,
  Your record I must know.
Your right and title must be clear
  Before you are allowed in here.

Come, answer quick, what have you done
  To be admitted here ?
What do you build your hopes upon ?
  I was a volunteer.
And proud I am, I wore the blue
  Fought for my flag and country too.

At Lincoln's call, in sixty-one,
  I joined the boys in blue ;
And like a bold son of-a-gun,
  Was to my colors true.
But of my valor, I won't brag,
  Through fire and smoke was with our flag.

VETERAN'S DREAM.—Continued.

Now please let up and don't be rough
  Upon a poor old vet ;
I own that I've been bad enough,
  But still I hope to get
Inside the gate and take a view,
    Meet some old friends and comrades too.

Like other sheep, I often strayed
  And left the shepherd's fold ;
By sin and Satan was betrayed,
  And left out in the cold.
I'm weary now of care and strife,
  And hope to enter a new life.

I own, sometimes I was headstrong,
  And easy led astray ;
I know I often did do wrong,
  And left the narrow way.
But now, I've changed, and to be brief,
  Have turned over a new leaf.

I never was a saint below,
  And neither a pet lamb ;
For with the boys, I used to go,
  And did not care a d—m.
I never lived up to the code,
  And wandered from the narrow road.

I am a pilgrim from the earth
  To seek a place of rest ;
My merits small, of little worth,
  And come here as a guest.
Go seek and find, thus said the Lord,
  I took the master at his word.

VETERAN'S DREAM.—Continued.

Saint Peter replies :—

My patience oft is sorely tried,
    With fellows on the beat ;
The good Saint Peter he replied,
    Come begging for a seat ;
They wear long faces—fat and sleek,
    And try to pass in on their cheek.

Bum Politicians, full of lies,
    Who spurn a poor old vet.
The boodle grabbers, d—m their eyes
    A fine scorching they will get.
Said good Saint Peter with a wink—
    They'll have hot brimstone for a drink.

No drafted men or substitutes
    Can ever enter here ;
Those scallywags and mean galoots,
    Must walk off on their ear ;
They want to ride on freedom's wave,
    And pass for heroes bold and brave.

No dastard sneaks, or lazy champs,
    Dead beats of any kind ;
No coffee coolers with the mumps,
    No quarters here will find.
Such fellows, we send to the hole
    And make the rascals shovel coal.

All bounty jumpers, cowards base,
    No room for them inside ;
You bet, they find a warmer place,

VETERAN'S DREAM.—Concluded.

Oh ! d—m them, let 'em slide.
With copper heads on the half-shell,
Will get it red-hot down in h—ll.

Now, some rich Scribes, and Pharisees,
 Who smite their breasts and pray,
Those fellows—they think they are the cheese,
 And own the right of way.
They rattle off long winded prayers,
 And think they'll climb the golden stairs.

Some people want to own the earth,
 They gamble, sell and buy ;
Will mortgage everything of worth
 And want to lease the sky.
They will get left, now you can bet,
 And what a tumble they will get.

My business 'counts not being squared,
 So I could not remain ;
Saint Peter handed me his card
 And told me call again.
With cheery hope and faith sublime,
 My boy, you're welcome any time.

Now, my old woman, she did scream—
 Get up you lazy turk ;
I then realized it was a dream
 And time to go to work.
Come, hurry-up, get out of bed,
 Breakfast's ready now, she said.

OUR CHAMPION.

Respectfully dedicated to JOHN L. SULLIVAN, by one who admires his
great qualities.

By Capt. P. KELLY.

I TUNE my harp in praise to sing
Our champion of the fistic ring,
Brave Sullivan from Boston town,
Fame's gladiator of renown.

In form, sublime, in action, grace,
True scion of the Celtic race ;
His country's pride—long may he reign,
And in the ring new laurels gain.

When forced to meet a vaunting foe,
And in the ring your valor show,
With nature's weapons in the square,
No armor in the strife you bear.

With Irish pluck and Yankee skill,
You're master of all champions still ;
My heart's best wishes, you may be
Each battle lead to victory.

Like Sampson in the days of old,
So lion-hearted, brave, and bold,
A man of muscle and great might,
You vanquish all your foes in fight.

May each new strife crown with succ
And victory all your efforts bless ;
For your proud heart the fates defy,
Would conquer death, and scorn to die.

TO MY FRIEND EDDIE MANN.

By Capt. P. KELLY.

MANN wants but little here below,
　　But wants that little strong ;
Like Gallagher, will let it go,
　　And takes it right along.

We're all poor sinners from our birth,
　　Then do the best you can ;
For saints are few upon the earth,
　　Just look at Eddie Mann.

To give the devil his just due,
　　And I don't care a d—m;
There 's many worse than me or you—
　　I'll shout for Eddie Mann.

A trusted servant thirty years,
　　He wrought for Uncle Sam ;
Through thick and thin and still appears
　　A bully little Mann.

Come, toast him in the flowing bowl,
　　This life is but a span ;
With all his faults, the good old soul
　　Is every inch a Mann.

TO MY COMRADES OF THE 99th REGI-
MENT, N. Y. S. VOLUNTEERS.

Written for the 31st Anniversary of our going to the Seat of War.

By Capt. P. KELLY.

A soldier's welcome, one and all,
We greet you to our banquet hall,
With love our hearts does overflow
For comrades thirty years ago.

What jolly times and lots of fun
Our boys had at Camp Hamilton,
There we learned the soldier's trade
To drill, mount guard and dress parade.

We welcome all, each mother's son,
Old comrades left from sixty-one,
It does not seem so long ago
Since we did guard at fort Monroe.

We hail with pride the days gone by,
When we dodged balls upon the fly,
And with the Johnies cut a shine;
Played hide and seek on picket line.

When we were pets of Uncle Sam,
Some villian stole our Colonel's ham,
And with his whiskey did make free,
It all was charg'd to Company E.

TO MY COMRADES OF THE 99th REGI-

MENT, N. Y. S. VOLUNTEERS.

Concluded.

Sometimes on scout we used to go
To forage and to meet the foe;
On chickens our brave boys did dine,
To have a feast in Ninety-Nine.

Some fellows they do shout and bawl,
To let them like a soldier fall;
Those snoozers don't know what it means,
Let them fall in for pork and beans.

I sometimes laugh and have to smile,
To see old comrades put on style;
For oftimes when they wore the blouse,
I've seen them chase a d—m big louse.

Our locks are thin and grawing gray,
My boys we have not long to stay;
And some are bald, but you can bet,
We thank the Lord we're living yet.

To absent comrades call'd above,
We think of them in peace and love;
And hope in glory bright will shine
Departed braves of Ninety-Nine.

NOTICE.

Persons desiring CAPTAIN KELLY's KNAPSACK can be supplied by Mail on receipt of price, or by Express, C. O. D.

Address,

CAPT. P. F. KELLY,

39 Beekman Street.

New York.

www.ingramcontent.com/pod-product-compliance
Lightning Source LLC
Chambersburg PA
CBHW022154020726
47496CB00008B/2704